To my past, present, and future kindergarteners, you inspire this story and have made me a better educator, writer, and person.

Thank you!

www.mascotbooks.com

The Paper Heart

For more information, please contact:
Mascot Books
620 Herndon Parkway #320
Herndon, VA 20170
info@mascotbooks.com

Library of Congress Control Number: 2019911314

CPSIA Code: PRT1019A
ISBN-13: 978-1-64543-016-2

Printed in the United States

The Paper Heart

Written by **Amanda Erwin**

Illustrated by **Bryan Madden**

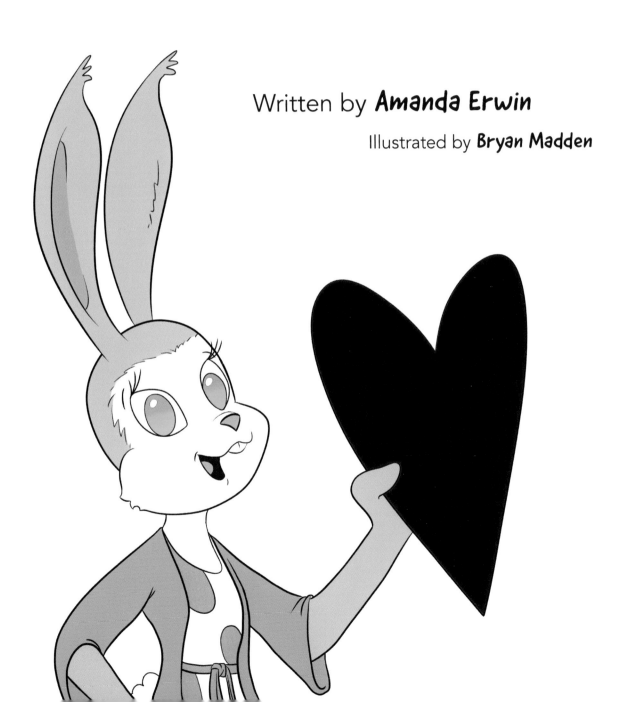

Mrs. Hare took a deep breath and walked over to Remey and Molly. "What's the problem friends?"

"Molly won't stop drawing on my paper!" replied Remey through tears.

"IT WASN'T ME!" shouted Molly.

Mrs. Hare watched the interaction as she had many times. Tattling and frustration had erupted in her classroom like lava from a volcano.

Her countless talks and reminders about how to treat your friends just weren't sinking in. Every time a problem came up, Mrs. Hare had to intervene and solve it.

Of course she didn't mind helping her precious students, but she had to teach them to be independent problem solvers so they could grow up to have caring hearts.

Wait! she thought.

That's it! Caring hearts...

The next day, Mrs. Hare called the children to the carpet for morning meeting.

"Good morning, friends!"

"Good morning, Mrs. Hare."

"I have to tell you, I was feeling pretty sad last night. I've noticed a lot of our friends are fighting and yelling and getting upset. And that breaks my heart!"

The critters lowered their heads and stared at the floor.

"But," continued Mrs. Hare, "when we have a problem, do we give up?"

"No!" everyone cheered. "We stick with it!"

"You're right! And I have something that will help us do just that!"

Mrs. Hare pulled a red paper heart out from behind her desk.

"That's it? A paper heart?!" The critters were disappointed.

"You got it, friends! When you look at this heart, what do you think of?"

"Yes, you are all right," said Mrs. Hare. "When we see a heart, happy thoughts come to our minds. Sometimes, we forget about how our heart feels. We let our minds and bodies get really frustrated and we never solve our problems. I think we need to start being more heart-focused."

A few critters formed their hands in the shape of a heart and pushed them out as if to say "I love this idea!"

Mrs. Hare continued. "The next time you feel sad, frustrated, confused, or angry with someone, I want you to come get this heart. Hold it up in front of you and tell them exactly how you feel. And, friends, if someone shows you this heart, get your ears ready to listen and your hearts ready to be respectful."

After Mrs. Hare showed the critters where the paper heart was going to be stored, she resumed class, feeling hopeful.

An hour passed without any issues, but suddenly Mrs. Hare heard **"STOP IT, MOLLY!"** followed by a **"I'M NOT DOING ANYTHING, REMEY!"**

Here we go again, Mrs. Hare thought. She watched with a quiet eagerness. *Will they remember the heart?*

STOMP, STOMP, STOMP, STOMP.

THUD.

Remey sat down on the carpet and started to cry.

Mrs. Hare sighed. *When will these critters stand up for themselves and share their voices?*

Mrs. Hare returned to her desk. She was about to ring the bell to get her class's attention, but she stopped when she saw something she couldn't believe.

Elliot, one of the class's most energetic students, approached Mrs. Hare's bin and reached for the heart. Then he walked the heart over to Remey.

"Remey," he said, "it makes me sad when you cry and don't tell us what's wrong. Here." He handed Remey the heart. "Do you want to use this heart to share your feelings with Molly?"

Remey snapped her head to the side and folded her arms. Elliot sighed, but Mrs. Hare gave him a big smile as he skipped the heart back to the bin.

"Good job, Elliot," said Mrs. Hare. "I don't think Remey is ready to share her feelings yet, but you did a good job using the heart to share yours."

After a few minutes passed, Mrs. Hare pulled Remey aside.

"Remey, you need to remember to listen to your heart. Elliot was brave to share his feelings using the paper heart. Remember, you can share your feelings and solve your own problems. Share your voice."

Remey nodded and walked back to work on her project.

About ten minutes later, Mrs. Hare heard Remey yell again.

"STOP IT, MOLLY!" she cried.

"I'M NOT DOING ANYTHING!" yelled Molly.

STEP, STEP, STEP, STEP.

Mrs. Hare braced herself for the **THUD**, but something different happened instead. Remey reached into Mrs. Hare's bin and pulled out the paper heart.

YES! Mrs. Hare thought as she watched everything unfold.

Remey slowly walked up to Molly. She held up the paper heart.

"I'm feeling sad and mad," said Remey. "I don't like it when you draw on my paper."

Molly stood there, surprised. "I thought it was funny," she said softly.

"It's not funny to me," said Remey, still gripping the paper heart. "Please stop."

"I'm sorry, Remey," said Molly. "I'll stop."

Mrs. Hare watched in awe.

"Friends, this is the magic behind the heart," said Mrs. Hare.

"Yay, the paper heart solved our problems!" cheered Elliot. "What magic did you sprinkle on it, Mrs. Hare?"

"The paper heart didn't solve your problems and I didn't sprinkle any magic on it, you guys did! Your words have the power to be magical. Our class just needed a little inspiration to use those magical words. When you can't get your mind or mouth to say what's bothering you, let your heart speak. Sometimes your heart can save the day.

Just remember, when life gets you down, upset, scared, or broken, listen to your heart and reveal the unspoken."

About the Author

Amanda Erwin is a kindergarten teacher and writer from Marysville, Ohio. She is passionate about inspiring children and adults to pursue their dreams and let their voices be heard. She is a loving wife to her high school sweetheart and dog mom to her two adorable pups. When Amanda isn't in the classroom or writing in her favorite spot, you may find her working out at her gym, traveling with family, or serving in her community.

A Note from the Author

If the magic behind the *The Paper Heart* has inspired you, please use this template to create a heart for your classroom. I hope it helps grow a sense of belonging and encourages your kids to use their heart to reveal the unspoken.

May you always teach with heart.

~ Amanda Erwin